This igloo book belongs to:

....

Contents

igloobooks

Published in 2016
by Igloo Books Ltd
Cottage Farm
Sywell
NN6 0BJ
www.igloobooks.com

HUN001 0916
2 4 6 8 10 9 7 5 3
ISBN 978-1-78557-686-7

Cover designed by Jason Shortland
Interiors designed by Chris Stanley
Edited by Stephanie Moss

Printed and manufactured in China

My First
Treasury of
Pretty
Stories

igloobooks

The fairy friends of Cupcake Wood
were happy as could be.
They had such fun as they prepared
for Honey's birthday tea.

They worked for **hours**, dusting flowers and tidying away.

Then, they all cried, "Oh! We forgot that Maisy's on her way!"

Everyone loved Maisy, but whenever she was there...

...she bombed the fairy beehive and got honey in her hair.

When Maisy's spells
made horrid smells,
it really was a pain.

She made a spell for sunshine, but instead it poured with rain.

Maisy waved her magic wand
to make a gift for Honey.
The spell went **wrong**, she made a mess
and no one found it funny.

8

Then, Maisy flew into the woods. "I won't use spells," she said.

"I'll try my best to use my skills to make a gift, instead."

Soon, everything was ready for the birthday-party fun.
When Maisy zoomed in asking, "Has the party tea begun?"

The birthday gift for Honey slipped and landed with a SPLAT!

"Oops-a-daisy!" cried clumsy Maisy. "How on earth did I do that?"

13

Cake splattered on the food, on sandwiches and sweets.
"Oh, no!" cried Maisy, sadly.
"Look, I've spoiled the birthday treats."

Poor Maisy felt so bad because she'd ruined Honey's day. "I'm sorry everyone!" she cried and quickly flew away.

"Oh, please don't go!" cried Honey,
as she wiped away a tear.
"I want you at my birthday tea..."

... but Maisy didn't hear.

The fairies mopped up all the mess and Honey dried her eyes.
She unwrapped Maisy's birthday gift and had a big surprise!

Inside, there was a pretty dress of gold and silver flowers. "Maisy made this," Honey said. "It must have taken **hours!**"

"Maisy can't do spells," said Honey.
"She always makes a mess.
Yet only someone **special**
could have made this lovely dress."

Each fairy's wings went droopy
and then Honey said, "I'm sad.

We've got to find poor Maisy, quick,
she must be feeling bad."

The fairies fluttered high and low,
in every glade and nook.

They found unhappy Maisy
on a toadstool with a book.

"Oh, there you are!" cried Honey.
"We've been looking everywhere.
We missed your crazy spells
and all the honey in your hair."

"I love my gift," said Honey. "Oh, please do come and play!
My party won't be any fun, if you stay away."

Maisy fluttered her little wings and giggled, happily.
"I'm so very glad," she said, "that you aren't cross with me."

Maisy laughed and had such fun and it was all because…

... her fairy friends in Cupcake Wood loved her,
just as she was.

10 Little Fairies

In the enchanted wood, the fairy bell rings.
Ten little fairies flutter their sparkly wings.

BrRRING

"Look at the time!" they cry and flitter away.
"We're late for Fairy School today."

Ten little fairies flying in a line.

One drops her wand.

POOF!

Now there are...

Nine little fairies at the fairy gate.

SNAP! goes a dragon plant. Now there are...

Eight little fairies say, "It's nearly eleven!"

BONG!

goes the fairy clock.

Now there are...

Seven little fairies practising their flicks.

ATISHOO!

goes a sneezy fairy. Now there are...

Six little fairies fluttering by a hive.

Bzzzz

BzzzZZ

"Yummy!" cries a greedy fairy. Now there are...

Five little fairies
by a magic door.

"What's in here?" says a nosy fairy.

Now there are...

Four little fairies come to a magic tree.

WHOOSH!

go the branches.

Now there are...

40

Three little fairies looking at the view.
WHOOPS! goes a clumsy fairy. Now there are...

Two little fairies, giggling, having fun.

NEIGH! goes a unicorn. Now there is...

One little fairy arriving at Fairy School.

Fairy School

She's all by herself and feeling like a fool.

Miss Sparkle waves her wand and suddenly, then...

one

five

six

seven

46

YOU AND ME ALWAYS

You're my best friend in the world.
You're always by my side.

You're there as soon as I wake up
and stretch my arms out wide.

The times I love the most
are when we play out in the sun.

Even though we're very different,
we have lots of fun.

Though you might like to have a
walk or chase after your ball,
you play the games I want to
and don't seem to mind at all.

We see amazing things
when we both go out exploring.

58

Nobody could ever say
playtime with you is boring.

You're brave as brave can be and
you're strong and fearless, too.
I know I can do anything,
as long as I'm with you.

When I'm feeling poorly and
I can't go out to play...

... we snuggle up together
for a cosy duvet day.

63

Sometimes when I'm upset
or I feel like I'm on my own,
your big, wet, sloppy dog kisses
show me I'm not alone.

I tell you all my biggest secrets
and my worries, too.

There's no one else I'd trust to keep
them safe except for you.

67

At night-time when it's dark,
you're always there to comfort me.

You make me feel so safe,
there's nowhere else I'd rather be.

As I fall asleep,
I hold you close inside my heart.
I love you so very much,
I know we'll never be apart.

Even Fairies Need Glasses

Cassie was a fairy who was quite misunderstood.
The problem was her eyesight, which wasn't very good.

It made her **very clumsy** and however hard she tried,
the magic spells she cast seemed to cause trouble far and wide.

Cassie needed to wear glasses, but the thought filled her with **dread**.

"I'm sure I will be teased," she thought, "with **those things** on my head."

On her first day of Fairy School, Cassie felt **really scared.**
"What if it all goes wrong?" she thought.

"I'm really not prepared!"

Whenever she swished her wand, it went...

...ZING!

PING!

POP!

There were
bursts, sparks and flashes,
then the teacher cried out, "STOP!"

"Cassie!" cried her fairy friends.
"You've messed up **every** spell!"
She didn't want to tell them
that she couldn't see
too well.

The next time Cassie tried, she was desperate not to fail. She meant to make a rainbow...

... but instead, she made it hail.

She cast **frogs** instead of puppies.

Her **potions**
all turned green.

The teacher thought her magic
was the **WORST** she'd ever seen.

83

Then it was time for flying class. "Get ready!" the teacher cried.

"Grab a pinch of fairy dust and spread your wings out wide!"

Cassie hoped and wished that...

...just this once she might succeed...

... but she fell SPLASH into a puddle...

... and felt very sad indeed.

Poor Cassie flew away. She gave a **sob** and then a howl.
"Oh dear, why are you crying?" asked a funny-looking owl.

Cassie sniffed and said...

Owl showed her **lots** of glasses,
everything from **big** to small.

Round glasses... ... square glasses...

... Cassie tried them all!

Suddenly, she saw some that were
all she'd ever dreamed.

They were **twinkly**
and **sparkly**.

They **glinted** and
they **gleamed**.

89

Cassie tried them on and straight away began to stare.

After seeing her reflection...

... she jumped up in the air!

"I can see!" cried Cassie. "These new glasses are just right."
So, she hurried back to school, full to bursting with delight.

From then on, Cassie's magic went **exactly** as she planned.

She had the **perfect** glasses...

... and the best spells in the land.

"Do that one again!" the whole class would start to cry, as Cassie swished her wand and pretty butterflies flew by.

93

By the end of term, Cassie was top of all her classes.
She could hardly believe it was all thanks to her new glasses.

"I'm **so happy**," said Cassie. "Whoever would have guessed that wearing my new spectacles would make my spells **the best!**"